This book is based on a poem inspired by MY FAMILY. I dedicate this book to my latest and greatest inspiration, my son, Chinua. The joy in your eyes when you open books and hear the stories, inspired me to write one for you, My Scoopable Chunk of Chocolate Love!

Good morning, Mama,
who was that on the phone?

Your grandma, baby,
she's stopping by our home.

"Why?" I asked
as she made breakfast for me.

She got a great deal on an outfit
and wants me to see.

"Why?" I asked
as I sniffed Mama's
famous blueberry pie.

Just Because that's
what families do. That's why.

So Uncle Shannon will pick her up
and bring her to our home,
because he doesn't want her to travel so far alone.

Now Aunt Sandy's coming
'cause she found a sale
on some chicken.
And you know how
Grandma likes to *throw
down in the kitchen.*

99¢ /lb

Then Uncle Chuckie
offered to cook
on the grill ...

... since Jasmine is home from college and just wants to chill.

Good news or bad times,
family is always there.
May not have much
But always willing to share.

Look!

Mauriqua arrived the same time that DJ did.

And they're watching Najee act silly, just like a big kid.

Then Marco stopped by
for no reason at all.
I guess he wanted to do
more than just call.

And Aunt Barbara traveled miles to show her support — Making sure we're still able to hold down the fort.

Maurice and Ray will be our DJs 'cause their music is groovin'
and Bobby gets the party going
when he starts to movin'.

So whether Sadiq wants to dance or Sue needs a hug,
we will open our arms and then *cut-a-rug!*

Great news! Uncle Cedric and his wife just had another son.
Time for a baby shower - now *those* are fun!

We're not perfect,
but we're perfect for each other.
For I can truly say,
"my best keepers are my brothers."

Through the years and the tears,
our triumphs and our fears,
in any situation, our family will come together.
The love we share only makes things better.

And this energy will continue for generations to come.
Through God and in each of us is where it comes from.
We accept each other and all of our flaws,
For the greatest love is family ...

Chiquita Camille Payne

AUTHOR: Chiquita Camille Payne is an Actress, Dancer and now author of her first book, JUST BECAUSE. Chiquita has been writing poetry for years, but her vibrant son inspired her to pursue book writing. Hence this is the beginning of a wonderful journey.

This native Chicagoan now resides in Brooklyn, New York. For more information, you can contact her at chiquita@chiquitacamille.com. or visit her on the web at www.chiquitacamille.com

Jerry Craft

ARTIST: Jerry is the creator of "The Offenders: Saving the World While Serving Detention!" a middle grade novel about bullying. He is also the creator of Mama's Boyz, an award-winning comic strip that was distributed by King Features Syndicate since 1995; making him one of the few syndicated African-American cartoonists in the country. He has illustrated and / or written two dozen children's books and games and has won five African American Literary Awards. His work has appeared in national publications such as Essence Magazine, Ebony, and two Chicken Soup for the African American Soul books. He also illustrated The Zero Degree Zombie Zone for Scholastic.

For more information, email him at jerrycraft@aol.com or visit him on the web at www.jerrycraft.net